For: Vicki, Lily, Edward and Tilly

Rockpool Children's Books
15 North Street
Marton
Warwickshire
CV23 9RJ

First published in Great Britain by Rockpool Children's Books Ltd. 2007
Text and Illustrations copyright © Stuart Trotter 2007
Stuart Trotter has asserted the moral rights
to be identified as the author and illustrator of this book.

ISBN 0-9553022-7-7
ISBN 978-0-9553022-7-5

Printed in China

rockpool
children's books

Stuart Trotter

Scaredy Cat

I'm scared
of monsters
under my bed,

And creepy-crawlies
fill me with dread!

I'm scared of flies,
and wasps,
and bees,

And even flying in the sky!

I'm really scared of barking dogs,

I don't like
holding slimy frogs!

croak!

Spiders in their
webs are scary,
Lots of legs,
all dark and hairy!

I'm scared I'll see a UFO,
Or fall into
the deepest snow.

I'm scared of
noises in the night,
Howling wolves
are such a fright.

I'm scared of rides at the fair,

I'm scared to comb my knotty hair!

Are there sharks in the pool?

I'm scared of the big kids
in my school.

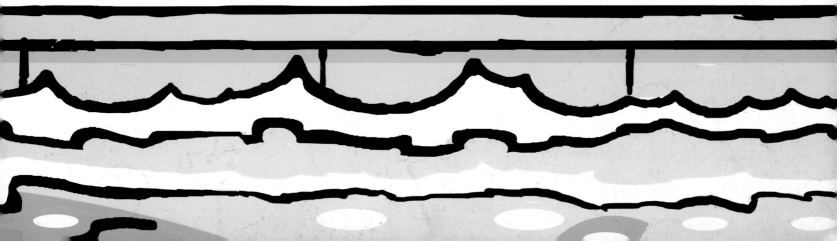

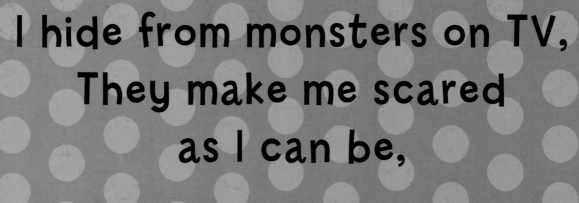

I hide from monsters on TV,
They make me scared
as I can be,

But everything
is fine, you see...

...as soon
as mummy
cuddles me!